14.93

WITHDRAWN

B R A V E

H O R A C E

by **Holly Keller**

Greenwillow Books, New York

Watercolor paints and a black pen were used for the full-color art.
The text type is Korinna.
Copyright © 1998 by Holly Keller
http://www.williammorrow.com
Printed in Hong Kong by South China Printing Company (1988) Ltd.
First Edition   10   9   8   7   6   5   4   3   2   1

Library of Congress Cataloging-in-Publication Data

Keller, Holly.
Brave Horace / by Holly Keller.
p. cm.
Summary: In the days before his friend George's monster movie party,
Horace prepares for the frightening events he expects will occur.
ISBN 0-688-15407-7 (trade).   ISBN 0-688-15408-5 (lib. bdg.)
[1. Fear—Fiction.   2. Courage—Fiction.
3. Parties—Fiction.]   I. Title.
PZ7.K28132Br   1998   [E]—dc21
97-5866   CIP   AC

For
my
brother

When Horace got the invitation to George's monster-
movie party, he made Mama read it three times.
"There will be popcorn, cupcakes, and a spooky
fun house," Mama read.

"I don't think leopards eat popcorn," said Horace.

"Of course they do," Mama answered. "And I'm
  sure they eat cupcakes. You'll have a lot of fun."

"And I won't be scared," Horace said.

"Of course not," said Mama.

At dinnertime Horace hardly ate a thing.

"What's wrong?" Papa asked.

"Nothing," Horace said, and he went straight to bed.

In the morning Horace didn't want to go to school
unless he could wear his dinosaur costume.
"Just this once," said Mama.

Horace plodded around the classroom and made
strange noises all morning.

He hid inside one of the stalls in the bathroom and
roared so loudly that the other children were afraid.

Mrs. Pepper tried to be patient.

The next day Horace announced that he was
an invader from outer space.

"What could be wrong with Horace?" Mama asked

Mrs. Pepper when she picked him up after school.

Mrs. Pepper shook her head.

At bedtime when Papa went to kiss Horace good night,

Horace was wearing his fake fangs from Halloween.

"I'm a vampire," he said, "and vampires don't kiss."

"What's going on with Horace?" Papa asked Mama when Horace was finally asleep.

"I don't know," Mama said. "But I hope it's just a phase."

"How much longer until the party?" Horace asked the next morning.

"Two more days," said Mama. "The party is on Sunday."

"Good," Horace said, "and I won't be scared."

"Of course not," Mama said again. "There is nothing to be scared of."

Papa looked up from his newspaper.

"At the moment, Horace, the scariest thing around here is *you*."

On Sunday Horace started getting ready for the party
right after lunch. He rubbed Vaseline into his hair and
made spikes all over his head. Then he sneaked up
behind Mama and growled as loudly as he could.

"Horace!" Mama shouted, and she dropped her knitting.

"Is it time to go yet?" Horace asked.

"Yes, Horace," Mama said, "it's time to go."

When Horace and Mama got to George's house,

George's older brother, Marvin, opened the door.

"It's not going to be a very good party," Marvin said.

"Lewis and Regina hate monsters, so we can't have

a *really* scary movie. And Mama made us take all

the rubber snakes and spiders out of the fun house."

"You mean there isn't going to be *anything* scary
at the party?" Horace asked.

"No," Marvin said, and he made a face.

Horace grinned. He smoothed down his spikes,
kissed Mama good-bye, and went bounding into
George's house.

The movie was good, and Horace ate a lot of popcorn.

He liked the mirrors in the fun house, too.

"Look," he said to Celina. "I'm six feet tall!"

"Look at *me*," Celina answered. "I'm a squiggle!"

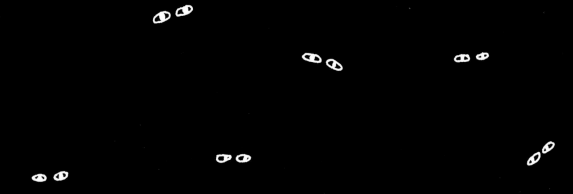

Then all of a sudden, just before they were going to eat

the candy and cupcakes, Marvin turned off the lights.

"I can't see anything," said Lewis.

"Me either," cried Regina.

"Stop it, Marvin," George yelled. "You're spoiling the party."

Marvin was wearing a mask with big green eyes

that glowed in the dark. He jumped up on a chair

and hissed like a snake.

"Anybody who wants to eat has to touch what's

in this box," he said.

"What is it?" Lewis asked.

"Monster brains and livers," Marvin said in

a scratchy whisper.

"But I thought there wasn't going to be anything scary," Horace said.

Marvin laughed.

Horace had goose bumps all over.

He didn't like being in the dark.

He tried to imagine what the monster looked like before his brains and liver got put into a box.

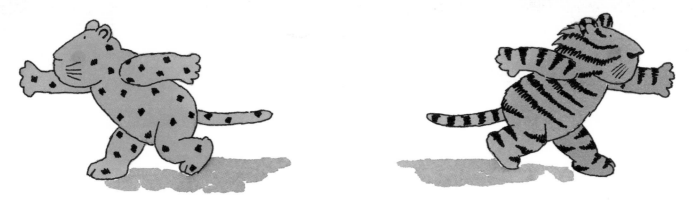

Horace tried to find the door. He slid backward slowly
along the wall until he crashed into Fred, who was
trying to find the door, too.

Fred screamed. Then Horace screamed.

"What a bunch of scaredy cats!" Marvin shouted.

"Come on, Fred, you go first."

"I don't want to," Fred said.

"You *have* to," Marvin said.

"No, I don't," said Fred, and Horace could tell

that Fred was about to cry.

Horace didn't want to go near the box either,
but he wanted to help Fred.

He wished he had
his vampire fangs.

"Scaredy cat, scaredy cat," Marvin sang,
and suddenly Horace was MAD.

"I'll go first," Horace said. He stuck his hand
into the box . . .

and George turned the lights back on. Horace looked

in the box. It was filled with green Jell-O.

"Some monster!" he said, and everybody laughed.

Horace and Fred each took two chocolate cupcakes
and a bag of candy.

"You were brave," Fred said, and Horace was happy.

"Did you have a good time at the party?" Mama asked
  Horace when she came to pick him up.

"Yes," Horace said, "and I wasn't scared."

"Of course not," said Mama, and Horace did three
  cartwheels in a row.